The Draugr

and other

Shadows of Decay

The Draugr
and other
Shadows of Decay

by Donald Cleave

Forbidden Books
Cambria, CA
MMXXV

The Draugr

and other

Shadows of Decay

by Donald James Cleave

Published by

Forbidden Books

Cambria, CA

MMXXV

Cover artwork by Katrina Mae Cleave

Interior illustration *The Dead Still Read*

by Jonathan Allen Cleave

Printed and bound by Amazon KDP

ISBN 979-8-218-58829-8

For Jonathan and Katrina
My inspirations for adventure.

The Dead Still Read by Jonathan Allen Cleave

Grant to life's day a calm unclouded ending,
An eve untouched by shadows of decay,
The brightness of a holy deathbed blending
With dawning glories of the eternal day.

A Hymn of St. Ambrose

Translated by J. Ellerton and F. J. A.Hort

CONTENTS

Introduction

One night after another barren attempt to write, I went out and stood on a favorite sea cliff and looked out at the ocean. The moon was conventionally full with a hackneyed shroud of clouds veiling a star specked sky. The sea waves crashed on the rocks at high tide several hundred feet below. I'd come here again to try to forget my struggles and failures, but the murmuring ocean brought no comfort that night. I looked over the cliff edge at the water-black rocks below and for a moment, I imagined myself readily falling into the teeth of those rocks and my blood splashing bright only to be erased in a moment by the churning water. The temptation quickly passed when my eyes refocused and I saw how close to the edge of that deadly cliff I was. I took a hasty step back. In that moment, I also looked out to sea and saw what St. John's Apocalypse might describe at the End. From out of the curling waves and rising from the depths arose the dead in their millions. I saw all those lost in that infinite sea suddenly called and coming to walk together on the water. The dead men and women and children lost in the ocean from that first cataclysm that Noah survived and all those since who have sunk below the surface. As far as my eyes could reach, I saw them in moonlight, all pacing solemnly towards the strand coming to greet me. This book is a collection that springs from that night when the dead came to me. In these pages, they come to you.

The Draugr

When the old ones went up taking blood to the elves, the white moon stood above the black well. Deep in the dark a figure in rags looked up with all hate at the eye of the moon.

Then rose the Draugr gathering its bones and the shreds of its skin. With cold pluming breath, fingernails splitting, tendons all creaking, it began to climb the wall of the well. Tendrils dangled from the rim of the well while rough laid stones cracked yet held and the cloud shrouded moon filled the circle above. Scaling and creeping, the Draugr ground teeth to sharding and splintering while joints pulled loose from all its flesh sacking. Yellow eyes burned with the corpse-light within till with soundless a scream the Draugr crawled free from its prison, the well.

On the rim of the well, the Draugr sat to take stock though the path was well trod. From the cliffs of the sea, to the well, then hoar-frosted heath to the strong timbered house that once was a home to the Thane and to She.

The house with its fire and its meat boards and mead and the red rustle beauty of raven haired She. All won and all spent after long journeys sought on the whale roads and ice flows and lands terror rent. When the ships swept ashore in the grey morning light and the bells signaled peace and of bread and of ale, the Thane and his reavers red-armed, blood sworn, brought them fire, to devour and to take. And then sword song whickered and whistled in air, iron brand danced, axe parted hair. Crimson leapt high from throat and from limb while the bells grew frantic, then, softly, then dim. The cries soon faded as the sun rode the day. The cattle were lowing, the sheep had all strayed. The silence then stretched from the ships to the town while the reavers stood panting, their Thane they now watched to see what he'd give. So, they entered a hall made of stone and all swept and coffer they found there that no one could lift and the Thane with a blow from war hammer struck and shattered the wards of the intricate lock. Then with eyes all around, he lifted the lid and flickering torchlight shone brightly on the contents it hid. Sharp intake of breath, the reavers took stock. It was gold, it was silver, both wrought and unwrought. With a signal, the Thane ordered sacks to be brought and the reavers staggered burdens that clinked in the cloth. And when the chest was broken and shorn, the Thane took the reavers to their ships and to home.

The Draugr sat watching the moon slowly passing its light caught the ice crystals on the heath gleaming and far in the distance fire light gleamed. The hearth fire burning in the home of the She. The Draugr then rose rotted rags all a-cloak. A journey, once more, to the house on the heath. The plunder had purchased the long-house and land. Then the gold and the silver were twisted to wire freely given and the reavers all praised and swore oaths and were loyal and one who a greybeard offered his daughter the raven haired, the dark of eye, the red of lip who kept the home in proud pride respect until the day the false one came in catching her eye and with boasts caught her ear. And the leather sack that was flush with gold lay open on the board with bread and meat and the drinking horn was passed and filled and the false one's eyes caught lust in flesh and lust in trove. The Draugr mused his word hoard pondering as the fire light grew closer and the sky was darkening.

The Sleep Thorn. That is what first made him think. The rune of sleep carved deep in a wood chip, noticed by chance as it fell from his bed. No matter, She often spoke elf chants and of thyme and potions mixed and herbs hung to dry. No matter. No matter. Then days had been parting, the false one stayed clear of spear-reach yet doubt still rested as rested the Thane and the delight of She as she sat on his knees when the shield-warriors saluted their Lord in his hall. She would pass him the chalice of mead wine mulled hot held to his lips and whisper "Drink deep and tonight I'll be thine".

The chalice was filled with witch-Dwale found in a dark book dragon skin bound. *Take thee three spoons of hemlock and juice of the poppy mix well three more of the henbane and boil then to sweeten add from the bee-eaters hoard and give to the one that will sleep as the dead and have done.*

So it was done and the unfaithful She and the false coward-one took him slumbering out and across his own land to the black well and there, straining against the great weight of his once muscled thews, strong arm, sword arm, limbs then unlocked, they dropped him into the well there to rot.

There he had lain for a year and a day until elf fires burned in the hills and the moon being right, he'd awakened and now stood swaying, at the door of the hall.

On the iron bound door thrice skeletal hand smote.

"Who be'est thou," a drunken voice spoke.

"Open." The Draugr breathed through the crack.

And the door opened and the false one, half dressed, stepping back.

But the Draugr was on him before he could speak. Long nails from bone fingers in the false one, dug deep. And the bright purple blood song poured from throat and from face then the Draugr shook droplets of crimson to the tiles while the hall burned bright with a fire at all peace. The Draugr then stepped over twitching corpse of thief.

Behold, on the meat board, now cluttered with filth, lay the bag of gold coins, what was left of the wealth. This the Draugr gathered up with his red spattered hands then softly he crept to a chamber within.

The ghost-light he cast made her beauty complete. White marble skin, limbs resting in sleep. Raven black hair spread sail-like unfurled. On furs she slumbered but in drunken repose. Her red lips hung open; her breasts all exposed. The Draugr stood silent at the bedside once his, then he opened the sack where the treasure lay hid and he scattered it gently on her stomach and hips. She frowned at its touch, then smiled in her sleep, thinking the coward had come more for to reap. Eyes closed, lips curling, she moved to one side, and the Draugr, the corpse Thane, lay next to his bride.

Bones in My Bedroom

When I was ten years old, I read Rudyard Kipling's *My Own True Ghost Story*. The story stood out in my mind over the years for the fact that, though Kipling builds us up with his descriptions so that we participate in his "fine fear", the tale ends with some disappointment. It lacks a ghost. Not to spoil Kipling's ending further, but his lesson stuck with me: there is always an explanation, and it is never supernatural. As I insisted on reading all things occult, this knowledge helped me until around 11pm when the solid fact that ghosts don't exist fades into a background of moving shadows. I became a master at arranging my sheets so that my head was safely covered while still allowing me to breathe. This skill helped considerably since my parents gently but with firm finality explained that I could no longer creep into their bed at the witching hour. Father himself made it clear that I was not to sneak into his bedroom no matter how scared I might get. I'm sure this had nothing to do with any romantic designs on his part but because he also had a penchant for ghost stories. In fact, on the last evening that I stood quietly by his bedside, he stayed up late watching *Night Gallery*. He slowly awoke to see my small figure illuminated by the moonlight. No doubt, the fact that I had wrapped myself shroud-like in my favorite white blanket helped stir his sleep burdened imagination as he sat bolt upright with a strangled gasp. Dad's quiet but firm ordinance from that moment forward was a genuine problem for me because my own room was haunted. Worse yet, I knew what I needed to do to appease the ghost, but I couldn't bring myself to do it. I wanted to keep his bones in my bedroom.

As mentioned, I was an avid student of the supernatural. The library in our small town didn't offer much beyond romance novels and boring "how to" deck building and garden books, but at some point, a librarian in charge had an interest in ghost stories. The library had at least four shelves devoted to the dead. I haunted those shelves reading and re-reading the books on them. Greasy to the touch with laminate covers peeling off like snakeskin, the books were filled with classic ghost stories. I fed on every one of them, but not just for diversion. At that time, I wanted to be an anthropologist and the folklore of cultures, especially their ghost stories, was research. What cultures believed and discovering the reasons why fueled my imagination. So along with the stories of the restless dead, I read about the rituals of headhunters in the Amazon and the temple sacrifices of the Aztecs. I poured over archeological excavation plans from England and studied black and white photos of the noose-strangled bog people from the Iron Age. I carefully read about L.S. B. Leakey and the skeletons he brought into the light. In fact, skeletons intrigued me. I wanted to reconstruct bone fragments like a paleontologist, maybe discovering that the cause of death was from a spear thrust with the flint spearhead still stuck in a cracked ribcage. Perhaps the reason for the death was to appease an angry ancestral spirit; the blood dripped over a grave to silence a banshee's cry in the night. Well ok, so the cultural traditions got a bit mixed, but it was all extremely formative material. What's more, I could participate in some of the mystery.

My childhood home, twenty minutes from a national park entrance, was wild country. Forests and cattle grassland stretched in every direction. Streams and ponds, lakes and marsh were all around me. A ten-minute hike in any direction could lead into a forest as dark as any the brothers Grimm walked in Germany. The mountains that loomed outside my bedroom window were once the hope of gold prospectors and one could find abandoned mineshafts without much trouble. It was a place of great beauty and great danger. Rattlesnakes lived under every rock, while black widow spiders spun in every dark corner. The haunted hills and woods around my home whispered adventure; a perfect place for a boy to get into trouble.

My troubles began with the words of my Auntie. Now Auntie was a bit witch-like in appearance with long curling black hair, dark eyes, and sharp features. Yet she was generous and very funny at times, and she could tell a good story. In hindsight, Auntie's one failing might have been that she believed every story she told no matter how improbable. But back then, I largely accepted her words as true. My ears fairly sizzled each time I listened to her yarns. One day as we sat at the breakfast table, she in fine form recalled an old well nearby where a fellow rancher found the skeleton of a young woman: True story. What might not have been so true was what she told us the rancher said, "Cows been drinkin' that water for years before they found her . . . and we've been drinkin' those cows' milk . . ." She said this after I set my own just emptied milk glass on the kitchen table. I have had a tough time drinking bone-building milk to this day, but that was Auntie and I always enjoyed my visits with her.

One afternoon while sitting with her by the fireplace, she began talking about the local Indians and the Ghost Dance. "The problem is we are the ones that done them wrong," she said. "The Injuns didn't need us comin' in an teachin' 'em and that's what made 'em mad. That and takin' what was rightfully theirs. So, they come up with the ghost dance. They'd dance around the graves all night on a full moon. They'd dance and dance right on the graves cryin' out for the dead to help 'em to kill us pale faces and drive us out. All night they'd dance until their bead necklaces broke and scattered in the dirt. Then they'd drift off at dawn."

"Where did they dance at Auntie?" I asked.

"Hmm, hmm," she hummed her humming chuckle. "Right up at the Injun graveyard of course."

"On Grandma's property? Up on the hill?"

"Right up there. How d'ya think we found all them blue beads we keep in the dresser drawer? We found 'em sprinkled round the graves right after the rains. Once, I even found a human tooth layin' up there."

"What did you do with it?" I asked.

"Threw it right down a squirrel hole. You know them holes lead right down to the coffins, so that's what's best to do if you find a bone."

"You should have saved it for me," I said.

Auntie shook her head slowly, "Naw. You best put them things back where they belong. We don't want the Ghost Dance to work, do we? Even though we got some Cherokee in us, we're still white skins to the ghosts." I may have been a white skin and of course I didn't want anything to do with a ghost, but then skeletons: That was something interesting.

A few weeks later, my class took a field trip to a local high school. This was supposed to encourage grammar school kids into thinking about a profession which we could begin to train for. It used to be that way where the grammar schools prepared one for the high schools which prepared you for a job in the real world whether it was working at a trade or perhaps even going on to college if you weren't going to farm. Things were different then. Anyway, we took this field trip to the local high school, and I was bored until we got to see the library which had a very decent collection, though we couldn't leave the tour and so I didn't get to see if they had supernatural or anthropology books; Disappointing. Then, after a sack lunch break, we toured the anatomy teacher's classroom. Now this was the best part so far. While most of the students crowded around a giant fish tank with the teacher's mascot, a one-eyed goldfish (one-eyed because a previous student poured a little acid in the tank as revenge for a poor grade), I stood reverently in front of a corner display case. As I peered into the case, the tired looking old anatomy teacher, a soft-spoken man who stooped a bit but still towered over me at six foot four inches, walked quietly up to my side. He saw me staring open mouthed at the skull.

"That's Chief Eagle Claw," he said. I stood looking into the case with awe. Chief Eagle Claw's remains, a perfect skull including jawbone, sat on the top shelf of the backlit case. The skull, bleached yellow white but with a touch of soil still clinging inside the eye sockets sat next to a less interesting dried sea sponge, a jar with the decomposed floating remains of a jellyfish, and various minerals and seashells.

"A real Indian chief?" I asked.

"Perhaps. I found him on a dig site up in the National Park. Back then you could keep such things. They only let me keep him now because I use him to discuss bone structure. Beats the plastic ones all to heck. You can see his sagittal suture perfectly here."

"How do you know his name?"

"Well, of course I don't young man. But everybody has a name, and I figured Eagle Claw was as good as any."

"How did he die?"

"I don't know. The skull was all I got at the dig. The rest of his remains were missing. Are you interested in studying medicine?" he asked hopefully.

"No," I replied. With that, conversation ended, but the image of that skull did not. I wanted my own display case with bones in it, but where to get the bones?

The ancient cemetery that lay on the edge of Grandma's property seemed like an amateur archeologist's dream. High on a windswept hill were the burial mounds of Indian ancestors. A few of the graves were still marked by weathered gray plank crosses standing at crooked angles amongst the rank weeds that grew there. The graveyard itself was not large and was roughly fenced with rusty barbed wire. I had been to this place many times and had even collected a few flakes of obsidian from arrow heads and the occasional blue glass or white soapstone beads brought to the surface by the rain. These things were always found outside of the fenced area as Grandma had warned us children to never enter the graveyard itself. "The land still belongs to them though they are long gone. We respect their place of rest," she warned. After seeing the skull of chief Eagle Claw, I found it harder and harder not to want to enter that place just to look down the many squirrel holes that dotted it. I never got up the nerve however and though I did hike up there one afternoon with a folding camp shovel, I feared breaking Grandma's trust more than any Ghost Dance. If only I could find a skeleton somewhere not so obviously off limits. I had no desire to dig a body out of grave though I had seen it done countless times on T.V., but I really wanted to study some bones just like a real archeologist might. We didn't have any Egyptian mummies lying around and we were lacking convenient Saxon burial mounds. I was too young to go away and participate in a real archeological dig, so where would I find a skeleton? My chance came unexpectedly on a bird hunting trip.

My father would often take me on weekend quail hunts. Most of these hunts were within a thirty-minute walk of my home and it was usually just that, a walk rather than a hunt; quail being in short supply. But I loved to get out and would follow behind my father's long stride as we made our way through the tarweed and sticker laden grass. I often carried an old single barreled .410 shotgun along with a buckskin pouch full of crackers and candy bars. Tucked in my belt, I had a genuine working tomahawk made for me by an uncle. I was ready for bear if one should ever show itself. One warm mid-morning, dad and I paused to share a partially melted candy bar under the shade of some oaks. As I sat on a stump enjoying the Hershey's, dad lowered his canteen and pointed further into the oak grove. "There is a very old burial ground over there; older than the one on Grandma's place. It was used by the early settlers that lived in the area; gold miners and maybe some Indians too."

I stood quickly and looked where he pointed. Under the lowering branches of the oak trees there was a single, blackened fence post riddled with woodpecker holes to mark the spot. "I don't see any mounds or grave markers."

"Too old," dad said. "Over time, the mounds settle and the markers rot away."

"Can we go look?" I asked with a growing excitement.

"All you can see, you can see from here," he replied. "Let's go home and get some lunch. It's too hot now for quail to be out." I noted the area in my mind, realizing that it was actually close to our home.

Weeks passed and I couldn't go out as much because of more than usual rain, but one day, I asked mom if I could go on a short hunt . . . by myself. Slowly, she agreed, "It's getting late so not for long and watch out for rattlesnakes and poison oak and don't go far. It's supposed to rain some more." And so, I was off. I made my way along a deer trail with my jeans getting damp from the rain still clinging to the yellowing knee-high grass. Though it took me a while to find the place again, the oak grove eventually came into sight. The graveyard was in a little valley with a creek bed running through it. I made my way along the deer trail and finally reached the trees below. It was gloomy under the oaks as clouds slowly passed across the sky. I found the weathered fence post and was soon standing in what I knew must be the graveyard. The grass was shorter here and the stream had rutted the ground along one side of the area leaving the red clay earth exposed. As I looked around, I was disappointed. No obvious graves, no blue beads, nothing but dead grass and a few ground squirrel holes with nothing to be seen within. It began to grow darker and far off in the surrounding hills, thunder rumbled. I knew I had to leave before the rain came so I began to follow the rutted stream course back towards the deer trail. The course was just caused by runoff, not a real stream at all, but the rushing water had cut deeply in a few spots and, as any good archeologist/geologist/treasure hunter knows, the exposed strata can reveal interesting finds. I walked along looking carefully. That's when I saw it. About halfway down the stream-cut bank, trapped in the clay soil but exposed to the world was a bone. Leaning my little shotgun against a nearby tree, I got down on hands and knees no longer worrying about the rain or getting my pants muddy. Jutting slightly out of the wall of the wash, a long brown bone followed the parallel lines of strata. I began to dig along it slowly, no ripping it out for me. I read about the care archeologists needed to take so as not to damage the find. I wished I had a trowel or a brush to gently clear the soil, but no time for it. As I worked, rain began lightly to fall, and the long grass bent and hissed as a wind came up until the oak grove began to sway and creak around me. I was careful though, not completely freeing the bone, but following it along. It took some time, but my work was soon rewarded, and I sat back with a gasp. Another bone followed in line with the first. I knew what they were too. It was a femur, and a tibia. The tibia was broken off on one end, but it clearly lay in line with the perfect femur. I had found my skeleton.

The rain began to soak my back, and the little wash started to run with water again and I knew I would be in big trouble if I didn't head home. So, leaving what may have been further buried, I carefully brushed off the two bones and clutched them to my chest running for home. I ran until my lungs were burning and my jeans were filled with foxtails and stiff with tarweed but as I ran, I knew what I would do. So just as my house came into sight, I made for an old oak tree just outside our gate. The tree had a deep hollow in it filled with sticks from an old packrat's nest: the perfect hiding place. I lowered the bones into the hole, and then slowly made for the gleaming back porch light just as night began to fall.

Mom was not happy as I had stayed out far too late and since my clothes were a mess, she made me strip nude out on the back porch much to my preteen embarrassment. However, after this humiliation, mom was not too hard on me since she had been raised on a cattle ranch and knew all about the mess boys could make. She sent me to shower then gave me hot bean with bacon soup for dinner which I wolfed down while poring over a book I had on paleontology. The diagrams of labeled skeletons inside told the tale and I was sure of what I had found, human leg bones. But how would I get the bones into the house and into my room without mom knowing? I knew she would not approve, few moms would, even moms who had been raised on a ranch. I figured I would have to sneak out at night to smuggle them in when she and dad were asleep. This was my plan when dad himself came home.

"So, your mother tells me you went out on a hunt. Get anything?" he asked as he heaved a log into our fireplace.

"No luck," I said faintly.

"Well, I hope you wiped the gun down if you were in the rain," he said, dusting off his hands. My guts went cold. I had left the gun in the graveyard.

Night comes early in the mountains and mom usually goes off to bed. Dad, however, liked to stay up a bit and read and that night the light in the living room seemed to stay on forever as I lay in bed pretending to sleep. Finally, down the hall, I heard dad yawn then the light clicked off and I heard him climbing into bed. He worked hard and I knew he would soon be asleep. Not so mom, however. Mom's usually never truly sleep I'm sure and can be awake in an instant. After waiting a while longer, I eased out of bed and then crept on cat feet along the hall that passed their bedroom. I had planned and had gotten into bed with jeans on. Only my shirt was nightgown for mom to see when she tucked me in earlier. I passed through the fire-lit house and eased out the back door without a sound. Outside, I put on my boots which were still mud caked from earlier and went on my way. My plans failed me though when I started towards the gate. The rain had stopped and there was a full and bright moon overhead, but I had forgotten to bring my flashlight. I would have a twenty-minute walk in the dark and I almost gave it up until I remembered the time I had left my new buck knife out in the rain for a couple of days and how dad had not been pleased. Dad was a patiently kind man, but he did not like negligence with new knives . . . or guns for that matter. I slowly passed the hollow tree that housed the bones and made my way carefully in the moonlight towards the graveyard. Of course, it was a long terrible journey, and I tripped once in a stupid squirrel hole. It knocked the wind out of me for a moment before I could continue, but after a while I dusted myself off and continued my night journey. After a long while, I finally came in sight of the oak grove and headed towards the tree where I had left the shotgun.

Although it was black dark under the trees, some moonlight was cast on the graveyard. The gnarled fencepost stood pointing at the moon like a burned finger, and I stayed clear of it, and I tried to avoid going under the brooding trees. I edged my way around, trying to keep the ominous fencepost in sight while watching my step. The thought flashed through my mind that there might be an open grave that I had missed earlier and what if I fell in? Even as I imagined this, the place came suddenly alive and I froze in terror when a sudden chorus of crk crk . . . crk crk . . . crk crk, echoed from the streambed. It was only tree frogs, but it sounded for a moment like the creaking joints of a hundred skeletons coming out of the earth. I quickly made my way to the shotgun, picked it up, and held it at the ready, only remembering then that it was not loaded. Another precaution dad made me take when I went hunting. No loading the gun until ready to shoot. I'd lost a lot of birds with this rule, but it made sense for kid safety, I guess. Now though it was horrible because all I had was an unloaded gun to point at the undead if they should appear. Still, it gave me confidence, and rather than going straight back, I foolishly edged my way over to the streambed and looked down at where the bones had once lain.

Water continued to trickle in the wash it had cut. As I watched it run, I began to think about that water having passed for a long, long time over the body buried there. The rain had fallen and finally cut into the earth and exposed the body. Perhaps the water had run over it until the flesh finally floated away in strips and then the hard bones were washed again and again until they softened until I found them . . . but not all of them. The rest of that skeleton was still there, tangled with roots; roots poking out of the ground like bone fingertips - moving like waving spiders legs tapping the crumbling soil; reaching for me. "Crk crk crk!" screamed the frogs and for the second time that day I ran like a deer for home with the frogs still sounding the alarm. I ran past the sentinel fence post and on through the dark thinking I could hear the skeleton dragging himself behind me coming for his missing bones. With my chest bursting I finally reached our gate where I stood gasping for breath. Behind me the hollow oak tree groaned softly in the night breeze, unhappy to be holding the skeleton I had torn from the grave.

Night terrors soon passed with the morning light and so over the next couple of days, I worked on the bones. Dad had given me an old cigar box that held the remnants of his own archeological interest from his college days. Inside was a dentist's stainless-steel pick, a worn toothbrush and a much folded and worn paper detailing an archeological dig in which he had participated. The box also contained what he had found in a fire pit he had helped excavate: a broken arrowhead, three shards of clay pottery, and the bone fragment of a quail someone had roasted over the fire a hundred years before. The bone fragment had some teeth marks on it where it had been gnawed by a Yokut Indian. Dad had chosen marriage and the honest work it required and so had given up his historical pursuits, but the box was one of my chief treasures. I spent a day dusting off the bones with the toothbrush and gently probing the ossified cavities with the dental pick. I then put the bones on display in the glass fronted bookcase that was part of an ancient desk that sat in my room. The desk itself was nearly a museum piece, made of mahogany that was black from years of cleaning with Old English furniture polish. The desk portion folded down revealing several drawers and numerous pigeonhole slots for letters and bills. I kept my paint set and other various treasures in the drawers as well as the cigar box. Standing back after closing the glass door of the bookcase, I admired the bones inside which I had laid on an old piece of red velvet. Since dad rarely looked in the case anymore and mom only dusted the outside of the desk, I figured the bones would go unnoticed. I was truly an archeologist now and the bones were ready to be shown, quietly to a few admirers; primarily, my best friend, Steve.

Steve lived an hour's jeep ride back in the hills from my house. Sometimes on a Friday after school, he would get off at my bus stop and spend the weekend with me then go home with his parents on Sunday when we would see them for church. One Friday, Steve did just this, and after having a sword fight or two in the back yard, I decided to show him the bones. I took him into my room after passing through the kitchen for some chocolate chip cookies mom had made. Steve was munching one now as he stood with me in front of the desk.

"Notice anything?" I asked.

Steve took a bite of his cookie, and some crumbs fell softly to the floor. "What?" he asked, chewing with his mouth open.

"There," I said, pointing to the bones.

"Your dad kill a deer and you got the bones?"

"No. I dug those from out of an archeological dig."

"Bull," he said.

"No really. Want to see them?"

Steve nodded, holding the cookie to his lips. I opened the case and took out the femur. "Be careful, they belonged to an Indian chief, or maybe a gold miner or a gunslinger."

Steve took the bone in his free hand, turning it gingerly.

"I dug these up near an old graveyard. This is the femur from the leg."

Steve stopped chewing. His pale face framed by brown curling hair was motionless for a moment. "Bull . . .," he said faintly as crumbs fell from his mouth.

I took the bone from him and put it back on its velvet cloth, closing the case.

"You better not do that," he said. "It's illegal."

"It's archeology, it's not illegal," I said. Steve's imagination had limits, and his reaction was not what I had hoped for.

"Your mom is gonna be mad."

"Keep it to yourself or I'll tell your mom that you smoked that cigar. And pick up those crumbs."

Steve shoved the rest of the cookie in his mouth. "Alright, cool. It's cool. Real bones huh? Let me see them again."

"No let's go out and catch a lizard." I pushed him back towards the door and Steve shrugged.

"Let's get some more cookies first."

"No more before lunch."

"So that guy's ghost is gonna come and haunt your —
if you keep his bones."

"Outside," I said pushing his back and he ran ahead
to the kitchen. I glanced back into my room just in time to
see a strange thing happen, the glass fronted door of the
bookcase slowly swung open. Maybe it was the breeze from
Steve running out. I walked back to the desk and pushed it
closed, then also hurried outside.

My sheets were twisted round my legs and the rain
had left the nights humid. The air was still and heavy even
with my window open and I wanted to get up and strip off
the old quilt that great grandma had made, but not tonight. I
kept a corner of it firmly wrapped up around my head with
only my eyes and nose exposed. My bed was under the
window facing the far side of my small bedroom. The desk
took up the wall a few feet from the foot of the bed and the
moon shining through the window reflected off the glass
bookcase that was part of the desk. From my bed, I watched
the desk. I had been dreaming of the desk which great
grandpa had sat at so many years before. In the dream, the
door of the bookcase opened ever so slowly. Now, awake, the
little alarm clock on my bedside table read 3 a.m. I had read
the book which the movie *The Amityville Horror* had been

based on and remembered that it was around 3 a.m. when the murderers had taken place in that demon haunted house. When I looked back at the desk, my heart stopped. The bookcase was open. I held my breath in terror and watched. Nothing happened. Sweat seeped out of my body and my head began to ache. I had to get up and cool off soon or I would be sick, but how with that case open? My flashlight was next to the clock, but I could not get up the nerve to reach out from under the covers and get it. What if something grabbed my exposed arm? I waited, suffering in the suffocating heat. Finally, I went back to sleep but was I asleep? From the distance across the hills, I began to hear what sounded like drumbeats. The beats were slow and matched the beat of my heart until I had to stop counting them because I thought if they beat the same, then my heart would stop when they stopped. I passed in and out of sleep in miserable heat-filled torture. The next morning, I awoke to the sound of mom in the kitchen, and I rose from my tangled bed with a slight headache. On the other side of my room lay the bones in the desk. The bookcase was closed.

Sometimes I would spend Saturdays on the ranch hunting squirrels with Grandpa or fish in one of the two ponds nearby. Saturday nights were the best because Grandma would stay up with me long after Grandpa went to bed. I would stay up till midnight and watch *Creature Feature* on Channel 26. Grandma would fall asleep on the couch long before the monster movies started, but sometimes Auntie would come over and watch with me. I now walked along the pampas grass lined path to her cottage. Auntie's cottage was nestled between some cottonwood trees in a little hollow not far from the main ranch house where Grandpa and Grandma lived. The whole property was some three thousand acres of cattle ranch and had several of these cottages sprinkled about originally for the use of the ranch hands that helped with the cattle. The ranch had been out of business for several years after the price of beef dropped and only a few cows roamed here and there on the vast property. The cottage itself, said to be over one hundred years old, had its own haunted history. Old Harvey Dix, a longtime ranch hand had lived in it till he died. In the tiny bedroom you could still see bullet holes in the wainscoting where he had shot rats from his bed with a .22 pistol. After Harvey had passed on, Auntie said that you could sometimes see a light on in the house though nobody lived there. Grandma said that it was because Harvey had put a Clapper on the lamp, and it shorted out sometimes. Eventually she disconnected the Clapper and rewired the house. This seemed to fix the problem, but perhaps Harvey's ghost had gotten bored no longer able to "Clap on Clap Off" and so had moved away. Not long after this, Auntie moved in.

Reaching Auntie's cottage, I knocked on her door. She let me into the small three-room shack, through the faded living room and led me into the tiny kitchen. I sat drinking a cold Coke while she made me a burrito on her potbellied stove, the only heat or cooking implement in the house.

"Gonna watch *Creature Feature* tonight?" she asked while sprinkling cheese on the burrito.

"Yeah, I guess so. Will you come?"

"Course I will. Vincent Price is gonna be in *Comedy of Terrors* tonight," she said with a humming chuckle.

"Auntie. You believe in ghosts, right?"

"Naturally," she said, handing me the burrito on an old plastic plate.

"How can you make them leave?" I asked

"Well. They usually haunt old houses and graveyards and such cause they have some grievance that needs settled. Like if a fella dies before he weds or gets murdered or if they killed themselves and then they go roamin' about trying to solve the problem. So, ya gotta solve the problem if you can."

"How about Indian ghosts?" I asked, cutting into the burrito.

Auntie pointed through the open doorway to her living room where I could see the corner of some sagging bookshelves. The shelves housed her chief treasures; a complete collection in twenty-three volumes of *Man, Myth, and Magic* by Richard Cavendish and a whole shelf full of decorative perfume bottles from Avon. "Professor Cavendish says that for restless Injun spirits you can burn some sage and then face the four points of the compass and ask the Great White Spirit to take the ghost to the Happy Hunting Grounds," she said. "But that prob'ly wouldn't work with the Injuns 'round here."

"Why not?"

"Cause the Injuns here in the hills was mostly Catlicks."

"What?"

"Catlicks. Roman Catlicks. You see, when the missionaries come, they brought hope and food to a lot of the starving tribes up here and so, being grateful and maybe a bit 'timidated, they become Catlick. They even built a little mission church over on the Drake Ranch, but they was still mostly buried on this place at the old cemetery. Remember them graves at the cemetery are marked with crosses? Old time Injuns used to just put their dead up on platforms open to the sky so their spirit could go right up easy. When the missionaries come, they stopped that practice and got buried in graves like the rest of us."

"What about Cat . . . Catholic ghosts?" I asked.

"Suppose saying some prayers or sprinkling Holy Water or somethin' maybe. Why you askin'?"

"Well . . . I might need to know someday," I said looking down at my burrito.

"Hmm, well don't mess with any of that exorcism stuff unless you plan to become a priest someday. It's all bad juju. Now eat your burrito and come out and help me find Yella Tail. He was limpin' round yesterday maybe got a foxtail in his paw."

The following week I spent concentrating on schoolwork. I was never good at math and Dad and Mom both took turns trying to learn me the basics of Algebra. They would have had better luck leading me through the ten spheres of the Kabbalah. After a day at school and a night of tutoring, I usually fell into bed in a dreamless sleep. However, a few times that week, I would sometimes awaken the next day to find the cabinet door housing the bones wide open. After about the third time of this, I took a white index card that I had been using to put the times tables on, folded it in half and wedged the door shut with it. It seemed to help until about a week later. I awoke late one evening to a booming sound in the distance which faded as I listened. It sounded like someone was beating a drum. My bedroom was pitch black on a moonless night and I slowly sat up and reached for my flashlight. Its chrome handle felt cold in my hand and my whole room felt cold. Flashing the light around the room, the light beam came to rest on the desk. The glass door was wide open. I slowly got up and walked on the tile floor around to the foot of my bed. The folded white index card was lying at my feet. I slowly raised the flashlight to look at the bones. Resting on the red velvet square, they gleamed in the light. A whisper sounded behind me and I turned expecting to see mom or dad standing in the doorway, what I saw was that my bedroom door had closed shut. I ran to it as fast as I could, bumping the corner of my footboard with my hip in the process and dropping the light. It rolled under my bed. I scrambled for the doorknob, but I couldn't seem to find it, the door was as smooth as a wall. I dropped to my knees and crawled partially under my bed, fingers outstretched and fumbled for the flashlight which had gone out. Thankfully, I quickly found it by touch and then crawled crab-like out from under the bed gripping the flashlight trying to find the on switch. On my knees in the dark, I switched it on. The beam fell directly on the desk and reflected off the opened door of the glass cabinet. In the glass of the cabinet door was a face. I thought it was my own reflection at first, but it wasn't me. The face looked at me. Long grey hair hung down framing withered cheeks marked with a thousand lines. It slowly faded and then was gone. My mouth opened in a soundless scream, and I leaped to my feet, found the doorknob, threw open the door and raced down the hall.

That Thursday and Friday night, I slept on the couch. Dad let me sleep on the couch in the living room next to the fire because I said I wanted to "camp", but I knew that would not last. On the night I saw the face, I told my startled parents that I had just had a bad dream from watching *Creature Feature*. Mom was set on telling Grandma that I couldn't watch it anymore, but I soon talked her out of it telling her it was my own fault. Ghost or not, I really didn't want to miss watching with Grandma and Auntie. But how long could this go on? By Friday, my back stiff and my eyes dark from poor sleep, I wondered what had I gained? I knew I couldn't stay out on the couch forever, but my room was haunted. I thought about telling Dad about it, but I was not sure how he would take it plus I already knew what he would want me to do. After lunch, I went into my room and stood in front of great grandpa's desk. I glanced around my room. Three bookcases held my archeology books, my collection of purple whiskey bottles found at an old mining camp, my rock collection arranged on one shelf and seashells on another. I had lots of cool things, and I had the bones in front of me. Opening the glass case, I lifted the bones out and studied them. They were smooth and kind of yellow. I had found them, but they didn't belong to me. They had once walked and talked as a person. Now that person wanted them back. The afternoon was getting on and soon it would be bedtime. I imagined the shadows in my room cast by the moon through my window stretching out to the bones and waking them. How could I spend the night here? Putting the bones back in the case, I made up my mind. I had to return the ghost to his grave. That night, I slipped out of bed and spent one more night on the couch. My only fear was that the ghost would glide down the hall and into the living room. Then he would take me with him. I wished I could slip into bed with my folks where I could be safe, but I didn't have the nerve to explain it all. I spent a restless night watching the fire die slowly in the fireplace and awoke the next morning with a crick in my neck and a sore throat, but I knew what I had to do.

After breakfast while dad was out and about and mom was working in the kitchen, I slowly took the bones out of the desk's bookcase, wrapped them in the red velvet and headed back to the cemetery valley. It was a warm day and soon school would be over, and summer would dry the hills golden. It was a good hike, and I even saw a couple of wild turkeys making their way down towards the creek I was heading to. I followed them slowly until they disappeared into the tall grass, and I soon saw the burned fencepost still standing alone under the oak trees. The little creek bed was also dry, and I went back to the spot where I had found the bones. I decided to bury the bones on top of the bank instead of in the streambed. I couldn't bring myself to go down where the rest of the skeleton's bones might be lying. I knelt at a spot roughly above where I had found them and dug the crumbing dirt with my hands forming a shallow grave. I laid the bones in carefully, still wrapped in the red shroud. After patting the dirt back into place, I stood over the mound, the sun hot on my neck. I looked around but the little valley was empty except for the silently watching oaks. Folding my hands I prayed, "Our Father, who art in Heaven, hallowed be thy Name, Thy Kingdom Come, Thy will be done, on earth as it is in Heaven . . . Amen" It's all I could remember. I scooped up some dirt and sprinkled it on the grave. "Ashes to ashes, dust to dust." The last grains of red soil trickled through my fingers. I felt my heart beating as I stood there, hands clasped in prayer and a warm wind stirred the air. Then

for the last time I heard them: Distant drums, drumming
softly in the hills.

A Tell Me Quick Ghost Story

Something was wrong with the bedroom. One glance around the dusty room proved that the new house was old and dirty. Andy's parents bought the house when they moved because of Dad's job and blah, blah, blah. So, the house was old, sure, but there was something else besides the cobwebs and the peeling paint; there was a smell.

Breathing in little wisps, Andy could just catch the odor. Not mold like under a leaky kitchen sink. Not empty tuna cans and banana peels left to stew in the garbage on a summer day. Nope, a different smell, and Andy knew what it was- the smell of a something dead.

A year or two before they moved, a mouse got stuck behind his parent's bedroom wall. The thing must have zoomed along a crawlspace and then fallen between the drywall where it couldn't climb out, like those stories of rats falling from rafters right into hotdog factory meat grinders. On hotdog days during lunch, the kids would sing. "My bologna has a first name, its M.O.U.S.E.!".

Anyway, the mouse kept rustling and clawing around all night until Andy's peace-loving dad, Herbert, would cry out, "Shut-up, shut-up, shut-up!" and throw shoes at the wall.

The mouse never seemed to tire, and the pattern of its scratching continued night after night. One day, Dad called Andy into the bedroom. Dad knelt in front of the mouse wall, unscrewing the plastic plate covering an electrical socket. A brown paper sack sat on the floor next to him.

"Got a little surprise for Mr. Mouse today, Son," he said, sweat dripping off his nose as he worked the screwdriver. "Open that bag."

Inside the bag was a green Bic lighter and a package that looked like it had AA batteries inside. Andy studied the package. In bright yellow letters, it announced, Atlas Chemical Company -Gopher Bombs POISON, followed by a cartoon rodent, belly-up, paws in the air, with little X's for eyes.

"Bombs?" Andy asked.

"Yesiree-Bob. Gopher Bombs," Dad said, tugging at some electrical wires.

"You're gonna blow him up? What about the wall?"

Dad shook his head vigorously as he tore open the package, removing a little battery-looking bomb. "No, not blow him up, though I sure wanted too last night." He handed Andy the lighter, a hungry smile plastered across his face. "You do the honors, Son. Light her up."

Andy carefully flicked the lighter."

A voice drifted from the living room. "Herbert, what are you doing to that mouse?"

"Mom," Andy whispered.

Dad licked his lips, his slightly bloodshot eyes glancing towards the door. "Nothing this little devil doesn't deserve!" he hollered. "We're just fixing the problem here, so don't worry about it, honey!"

"Why don't you let it alone? It'll probably just die on its own anyway. Poor little thing."

"Poor little thing. Poor little thing's a pain in the aa... -uh, neck," Dad muttered, glancing up.

At that moment, from behind the wall. *Scritch, scratch. Scritch, scritch, scratch.*

Andy and his dad listened, then raised their heads slowly until they were nearly nose to nose.

A muscle twitched in Dad's cheek. "Light it," he said.

After a few flicks, the lighter sparked into flame. Andy touched it to the little fuse sticking out of the bomb.

"Fire in the hole," Dad said, showing all his teeth like a jack-o-lantern, and dropped the bomb in.

Andy stuck his fingers in his ears.

Nothing happened. No firecracker boom, only a pause, then curls of smoke drifted out of the electrical socket.

"See, kills 'em with poison smoke." Dad explained, still grinning.

The smoke thickened, stinking like rotten eggs.

Dad leaped to his feet, ran to the bedroom window, and slid it open with a bang. "Better head outside for a bit Son, until it clears!" he shouted. "We got him though. You betcha we got him!"

"Herbert? What's that smell? Herbert!"

***

Andy smiled at the memory. They got him alright, but the smoke wasn't the end of it. They knew the bomb killed the mouse because a few days later the mouse started to rot. The smell made you gag, and it grew as another warm day passed. Deep, rank. 'Cloying' was the word Mom used. Dad used other words.

Finally, Dad hired a guy to cut into the wall and remove the mouse. The once tiny body had swollen like a dandelion puff ball. The guy dropped the body into a black trash bag, then, with a disgusted look on his face, reached back into the hole and drew something out. In his hand he held the blackened stub of the gopher bomb.

***

So, it must be a dead mouse.

Andy scanned his own bedroom walls. The plaster had a few fine cracks in it, but no holes. Maybe below the floorboards. He shifted his weight from side to side. The hardwood under his feet gave slightly. Crouching, he looked under the bed. Nothing. There was nothing dead in the room.

***

That night, the wind blew in a rising storm. The house creaked and groaned. Andy opened his window a crack and the long, white drapes stirred with each gust, casting moving shadows.

Andy tossed and turned in the little bed. After a while, he rolled over and peered at the Darth Vader clock on his nightstand. '11:40pm' glowed digitally in red across the Dark Lord's chest. Almost midnight.

It's twelve O'clock- the witching hour.

The witching hour? Where the heck did that come from? Then he remembered. He'd read a stupid comic book called, *The Witching Hour* at a friend's sleepover.

On the comic's cover, an old hag glared her yellow eyes and grinned her snaggled teeth. She pointed a long, crooked finger at a clock striking midnight. Andy remembered the story too. A guy made a witch mad, so she put a hex on him at midnight. Witches cast spells at midnight when things got thin between our world and the ghost world. Ghosts would rise and help the witches.

In the comic, a witch stood with arms stretched over a black cauldron. Ghosts swirled around her in a green mist with mouths gaped open.

Andy pulled the bedcovers up to his chin. The thought flashed of going to his parents' room. Dumb. Go crying to mommy and daddy for no reason. He wasn't a little kid anymore.

No, but maybe he could just check on them. Adults checked on kids sometimes, why couldn't he check on his parents?

Easy. Just head out of his room and up the stairs and through the living room, then down a long hall and finally, to his parents' room at the end.

Quite-a-ways. He would need a flashlight. No good, that was somewhere in the packing boxes. Everything was packed, even some furniture still draped in sheets.

Why cover chairs with sheets? Dust. That was it. They didn't want to get dust on stuff. Andy listened to the wind and imagined it blowing through the sheets.

He pulled the covers up to his eyes, then over his head. It felt better underneath, like in a tent. He made just enough of an opening so he could breathe, then closed his eyes, and began to count. Before he reached two hundred, he fell asleep.

***

Andy blinked, then he retched. The smell of rot choked him so he could hardly breathe. He sat up, one hand over his nose and mouth trying to block the horrible stench that rolled over him. He tried to scramble out of bed but felt trapped as if in a small space, his legs pinned. Where was his clock? He couldn't see it. The room was pitch black. And then, there was a light. Andy watched it grow, his heart hammering.

The light: a smooth, oval of light floated like a balloon. But Andy knew it was not just a light, it was really a face - a pale, glowing face with eyelids closed. The face was small, like a kid's face and it drifted closer and closer, and all Andy could do was watch until the pale, soft face was only inches from his own and then slowly, slowly, like someone coming awake from a long sleep, the face opened its eyes. But there were no eyes, only empty pits staring in the darkness. And then the face smiled and opened its mouth, and the lips whispered something on breath as rotten as the grave.

***

The next morning, Andy dug through boxes until he found his flashlight. Batteries almost dead, the flashlight emitted a weak brownish beam, but he couldn't find any fresh batteries in the boxes. Finally giving up the search, he stuck the flashlight in his jacket pocket, went outside and sat moodily on the swing in the backyard.

Rusty chains suspended the cracked swing seat still wet from the night's rain. Ignoring the damp patch the wet swing made on the seat of his pants, Andy thought about the face in his dream. Moments after the face opened its eyes, it disappeared and so did the trapped feeling. Andy had leapt out of bed and ran upstairs to his parents' room. No, he didn't go in and wake them. He just stood for a moment in front of their bedroom door, then slept on the couch, covering himself with a dust sheet. The funny thing was, Andy didn't remember waking up from the dream, just getting up and heading upstairs. But it had to be a dream. Had to be.

Maybe it was something he ate like Scrooge in the "Christmas Carol". He thought of what he had for dinner. Soup. Just soup and bread since Mom didn't have all her pans unpacked yet. Cookies! He ate some cookies before bed. Those striped chocolate cookies made by the elves in their cookie tree. That might have been it. No. it had to be the *Witching Hour*. That stupid comic book he thought about, and the dead mouse in the wall, and the smell, all that made him imagine the whole thing. Had to be.

Andy glanced around the yard. Besides the rusty swing set, there was nothing to see. Just an elm tree, a rusted-out wheelbarrow, and a ton of ivy growing everywhere. The ivy, glistening with raindrops, climbed the house. Dark green tentacles swarmed up the walls, right to the roof. Bored with the ivy, and sick of the wet swing seat, Andy decided to go back inside, then he saw the little door.

The ivy didn't quite hide the door that led under the house. At some point, someone had pulled free the clinging vine and Andy tore off even more and then pulled the door halfway open. Getting down on his hands and knees, he snapped on his flashlight and peered inside.

Nothing in there. Just dirt and webs. The flashlight's shaky beam didn't reach far, and Andy decided not to get all dirty for nothing, but then he remembered the smell. Yep, he could smell it under there too. Maybe he could find the dead mouse if that's what it was, and Dad could get it out so it wouldn't stink up his room. Unless it was something bigger. What if it was a dead cat? Better not to think about that, but whatever was causing the stink he should have found it because this little door was right under his bedroom. What if it led to a trapdoor into the house? Old houses sometimes had that stuff built in. What a surprise for Dad, if Andy popped out of a secret door! With this possibility bringing a smile, Andy pushed the flashlight in front of him and crawled through the door.

The smell grew and so did the dust. Choking clouds of dust stirred up as he crawled on the dirt floor. Andy hurried forward, hoping to leave the dust, but he ran right into a gauze of spider webs. Clawing at the webs draped across his face with one hand while clutching the useless flashlight in the other, Andy tried to turn around to go back, but as he turned the soft dirt under him gave way and he slipped forward and down, sliding into darkness.

Andy landed on his knees in soft, powdery dirt, so he wasn't hurt, but he couldn't see a thing. He lost the flashlight. The light went out. Worse though, he could hardly breathe from the dust he stirred up during the fall. He pulled up his shirt and ducked his chin so he could breathe through the cloth which helped, but what was worse than the dust was the smell.

The smell, the stinking rot-smell churned around him in waves, choking his every breath. He'd fallen into a pit under the house or maybe a dry well. Couldn't be a well, he hadn't fallen too far down. A pit then, but where was the flashlight? Feeling the ground in front of him, Andy felt something like cloth and jerked his hand back. Something like a bundle of rags was in front of him. After a moment, the dust had settled enough for him to breathe, so he cautiously felt around on the ground to his right. His fingertips brushed cold metal. The aluminum handle of the flashlight! He grasped it and flicked the switch. No light. He banged it on the ground, flicking the switch on and off. The feeble beam flickered on. Andy pointed it towards what he'd touched.

A tennis shoe. Grey sweatpants. Legs. One leg outstretched, the other bent at a sharp angle to one side. A ragged tee shirt with stick-thin arms poking out of the armholes. And then the head.

A small, round head, leaning back against the dirt wall as if it was resting. Resting but not sleeping because the eyes were open in the pale, pale face. Eyes that were just black pits staring from a gaping mouth lined with little teeth. And as Andy drew a deep breath to scream, the rotten smell of the dead boy rolled over him. And as the flashlight batteries finally drained, the brown beam of light faded out but the face in front of Andy glowed with its own phosphorus corpse light and in the final darkness, the smooth, oval of light began to rise like a lazy, drifting balloon.

Take My Hand

Where did I meet James? Well, if I remember correctly, it was while waiting in line at the Fisherman's Wharf Torture Dungeon.

No, No, come on, not that. You know, a Torture Dungeon. Like the Wax Museum tour or Ripley's Believe it or Not -Like a funhouse. You basically go through a series of rooms staged with various scenes depicting medieval torture. James was in front of me in line and when he went to pay for his ticket, he dropped his wallet. I picked it up and handed it to him and . . . well, yeah. That's how we met. We struck up a conversation during the tour, what? No, you can talk, it's not like a play or something. You go in from room to room and . . . No, like I said, it's just cheap animatronics and painted on blood. Different scenes, like a guy in an electric chair where you put in fifty cents and lights flash and his eyes pop out. Not really. No! It's just a dummy and the eyes are on springs or something and go back into its head when the thing resets for the next customer. That kind of thing throughout. Why is this so important?

Well, I can tell you if it's necessary, Counsel. As much detail as you want. One room had witches flying around on brooms and then one witch was getting dunked in a barrel of water, being tortured, while in the same scene, three more witches were getting burned at the stake. No, not real fire. It was orange and red plastic fire cut outs with fans underneath them to blow them and then a soundtrack of the crackling flames and the witches screaming, and.. . . What? Were we into it? What do you mean? I don't like that implication. Listen, I know you've been appointed for me, but what's with all these personal and frankly disgusting implications you're making? No, I think you are. Yes, I understand that your job is to defend me, but I'm here voluntarily. I'm not under any suspicion. This is routine at least that is what I've been led to believe or I wouldn't have come down here. I'm here to help since James disappeared. But you know, I think he just left on his own. So... Okay, fire away. As personal and nasty as you want.

James and I were, are into classic horror. For instance, we started talking about Barbara Steele when we got to the torture room with the iron maiden in it. Oh, come on -an iron maiden – you know – like a big steel coffin but with spikes inside. When the victim is put into it and they close it, the spikes go in, the spikes puncture into the victim. Well, James said he loved that scene in the movie *Black Sunday* where they put a mask with spikes in it onto Barbara Steele, the actress, when she is accused of witchcraft. . . No, no, listen, I'm not going to describe it all to you -just go see the movie. No, like I said, I want to help. I'm not being difficult, but you're basically asking me to describe the foundations of the gothic horror genre and . . . Yes, Barbara Steele is an actress and is rightly considered the ultimate British scream-queen and if you don't get it, then go look it up for yourself.

Okay, I'm sorry, but. Okay, sure. James and I joked about the various torture scenes as we went through the tour. They had another one of this guy getting so-called Chinese water torture. Huh? Oh, so called because the Chinese didn't invent that torture where the victim is strapped in a chair then water is dripped on his head one drop at a time for days and days drip, drip, drip, drip, until the person goes crazy from it. No, the Chinese had nothing to do with it. That type of water torture was first mentioned by an Italian lawyer named Hippolytus clear back in the 1500's. Yeah, then the magician slash escape artist Harry Houdini, and please don't ask me who he is. Yeah, Houdini, well he popularized the whole thing from one of his shows where he would escape from what he called a Chinese torture cell and back then, if you wanted something to sound magical or mystical, you made some connection to the Orient, so calling it Chinese torture back then was mysterious.

Anyway, James was interested in that one and he asked if I could imagine being strapped down for weeks as the water dripped on my head one drop at a time, drip, drip, drip and after a while you start to anticipate each drop falling and falling, a tiny little drop of water and then 'ping' it drops onto your head and then again and again and again, always in the same place on your head until each strike begins to feel like a pin pricking your scalp and then, maybe after the thousandth drip, the pin prick becomes a nail being driven into your skull, tap, tap, tap and you know it's coming and that drip becomes an agonizing pounding; wham!, wham! wham! A sledgehammer striking your skull for an eternity, but it is just that little drop of water that you can see in your mind's eye falling, falling. And then, you break, and you confess your crimes -that is what Hippolytus the lawyer was interested in. Hah. Hah! You too maybe, huh Counsel? Got any water handy? How about that dixie cup of water there for starters huh? Hah!

Yes. Understood. Getting slightly off track or off 'rack' I should say. How about that? Get it? Off rack? You would probably be more interested in using the rack to stretch the information out of me. Am I right? Ha! They had a silly set-up for the rack scene at the torture chamber. The dude on the rack was all stretched and twisted like Gumby and his papier-mâché tongue was hanging out of his mouth, his lips all twisted in pain. Silly really.

Oh, that's silly too. Of course I don't advocate torture for getting confessions from suspects. Give me a break. Let's wrap this up. After the torture chamber we went to lunch and discovered that we both liked Indian food -good spicy curry. A week later we -huh? I don't remember the specific date. Just seven days or so after meeting at the Fisherman's Wharf. Yeah. Make it eight or so days, it was a Tuesday. Yeah, so we went to lunch again and we met off and on for a month or so. No, I never saw his place, we always had lunch or dinner or whatever in town and. Well, yeah, so then he ended up moving in. My place has a guest room and... Well, again, that's really none of your business Counsel. And really, I'm about done here I think anyway, though I think we've both wasted our time.

Our personal relationship is not on the table, I thought I made that clear. For the record then, okay, for your record just write down we were like Holmes and Watson. Oh, come on, surely you know – yes Sherlock Holmes just right that down. You don't get the connection? Counsel, you really need to read. No, read books, real books not law books or shrink books since you say you're a psychologist as well huh? Oh, criminal psychologist. Well, why didn't you say so? You conveniently left the 'criminal' part off when you introduced yourself.

And that's the bottom line, isn't it? I'm here as a suspect just because he was my roommate. He just left. He took off. Greener pastures and all that.

I never met his parents. He never talked about them. No. I don't know how they knew he had been staying with me. He must have told them at some point. Phone, mail, text, I have no idea. Like I said, I had no knowledge of them until you people showed up and said they had reported him missing.

He moved out about a week ago. Nope, not a word to me. I just came home and noticed he was gone. Out I thought, until a day or so passed, and he didn't show up. He never said he was leaving, he just did. Like I said earlier, about two weeks ago. No, it never occurred to me to report him missing. He's a grown man and can take care of himself or so I assumed.

Well, you said too. You said to take it.

What? I'm sorry. No, I just thought I heard someone. Outside, I guess. What? No, wait. It was just something I remembered from the Torture Dungeon. It's not important. All right, all right, sure you decide, but it was nothing. At one point in the tour... yes, the dungeon tour, what we're talking about! No, but it's...No, I'm not distracted. So let me tell you then. At one point there's a long hallway leading from one room to another and it's pitch black. You have to sort of feel your way through it and at one point you said, 'Take my hand'. Just something I remembered that I...No, you did say that. What? I'm sorry Counsel, but you said... I mean... Hey, I need a break. Can I have a break or something?

Okay, I'll finish the part about the hallway but then I need to go home. Got it? I shouldn't even be here.

So, we um. Well, we get into the dark hallway, and I feel his hand on my shoulder for a second and then he, hah! We stopped and he put his hand on my face and that's when I noticed the ring. Yes, he touched my face. My cheek. He had a ring on. It was cold. Later he showed it to me - it is hard to miss the thing. It was a high-quality reproduction of the ring Bela Lugosi wore when he played Dracula. Big stupid ring. Real silver with a Carnelian stone with a made-up heraldry for Dracula also in silver. Carnelian is reddish orangish brownish. You called it a bloodstone. Dumb. It is dumb. Why wear such a thing. Counsel? I ... I am addressing you. What? I doubt it. I really doubt it. It was just a reproduction. A quality one yes, but not the real prop Lugosi wore. That would be worth, I don't know thirty or forty thousand. Yeah, dollars. Come on Counsel.

Why did you put your hand on my cheek? I'm just thinking out loud. What did he say after that? He said to take his hand. Yeah, in the dark, to...to lead me through the dark. He gave it to me then. Huh? No, his um, his hand. His...No, not the ring. Oh. Hah! Yeah, there you go Counsel! I wanted his Dracula ring. There's your motive. Hah, hah, hah! Oh, exactly. That's it. I coveted his original -oh yes you did say it belonged to Lugosi! You said it. Liar! And then you -he – take – take my hand…I won't. I won't give it back! Never.

**

Why wasn't a regular search performed when they brought him in? Ahh that's right, he came in when your people called him. Voluntarily then? Okay. And the story wasn't all true because he had known James for a couple of years, right? Lived with him for a couple of months then called his folks asking him to stay with them because he was moving out but two weeks later and no contact and that's when they called missing persons. All they had was an address. Okay, so the story of how they met was true but had taken place two years ago or so. Told it pretty. He was cool as a cucumber till the end, wasn't he? Only till the end there. And later he said that he literally saw the victim standing in the room during the interview too. Well, it's up to the shrinks now then. Never get a murder conviction against him if he was arguing with a ghost during the interrogation. Crime of passion or something maybe. Based on the evidence, right? Twisted love. Though he said something different, they clearly were into weird stuff. All that horror movie business.

Well, it couldn't have been greed because the ring was just a reproduction like he said. Yeah, real silver, genuine bloodstone setting etc. but not owned by Bela Lugosi. Oh, maybe a couple of hundred dollars is all it's worth and he had that in his jacket pocket that whole time? And after he finally calmed down, they found it when they searched him -right in his jacket pocket. I wonder how long he had been carrying it around? Forensics will figure it out. But still, unbelievable - the victim's left hand with the Dracula ring still on its finger.

The Librarian's Daughter

For a moment, she forgot to breathe. The answer rose like a ghost from the faded script. Rebecca closed the book, slid it into her bag, and left the library.

Outside the city lights reflected, stretching shadows. The day's rain made black mirrors of the streets. Rebecca clutched her collar, her eyes following the marching streetlamps. The city at night in the Old Quarter. Always so romantic.

Dizzy, happy, on red wine. After dinner at that French restaurant. He danced with her under the streetlight.

"Cobweb thoughts leave me be," she whispered, shaking her head. She started walking slowly at first, then faster, her heels clicking echoes on the wet sidewalk, the bookbag bouncing on her hip. She slowed, shifting the heavy bag to her other shoulder.

How could he?

A stupid question. The man was a drunk. Drinking and drinking while she worked, trying to make ends meet until what? No more credit, no more cash, Mom's stuff all sold. Two years and never enough.

How 'bout those old books, Becca? His tongue swept wetly as he formed the words.

Damn him! Where could he have sold them? Maybe some pawnshop owner with a keen eye. No, probably one of the bookshops. Rebecca imagined the sudden ache of book-lust falling on a buyer. 'Arkham House First Editions?' he'd ask, already knowing, slowly turning, opening, fondling. Her books. Jack's hand reaches out for the money.

Oh, those books! She'd worked and saved, hiding what money she could. One by one, she'd collected the dark titles. At first, she bought the Arkhams because of their curiously illustrated dustjackets. Later, it was for the stories inside the foxed pages. Those writers all shared something - twisting worm thoughts.

When Jack passed out, Rebecca read the stories over and over, drifting into eldritch landscapes and haunted halls where women in sweeping gowns of green velvet descended staircases at midnight. Children peeked into crumbling wells and rooted around the gravestones. Dark-eyed men with skin like porcelain sat in mahogany studies surrounded with books that climbed the walls like ivy.

And Jack went to the shelf, boxed them up, and sold them.

Novocain lips. She remembered that. When she saw the empty shelf, she clearly recalled a tingling numbness as the blood drained from her face. She screamed. Jack laughed.

Jack's laugh. The laugh that turned heads in a room, and when people heard it, they laughed too, joining in with the fun of it. Booming laughter so full of good, drunken cheer.

Laughing, Jack went upstairs to drink and to sleep, and Rebecca went into the kitchen and opened a drawer. Neatly folded inside the drawer was a turkey roasting bag -a big, plastic oven bag to cook the Thanksgiving turkey in. A basting bag, with a long, yellow zip-tie. Why so long? Rebecca didn't know, but there they were, the bag and the tie, all ready for Thanksgiving. Mom said a turkey roasted in a bag retained its juices. Mom used that word -retained. Retained its juices.

The white and green house with the white picket fence was a short walk from the library, which was good, because it might rain again. Fifteen minutes of brisk walking brought her home. A light shone warmly through the curtains of a downstairs window, an old habit of Mom's. *Leave a light on in case you get home late.* The upstairs window was dark.

After opening the little garden gate, Rebecca followed a mossy path to the front door. She dug her keys from the bottom of the bookbag. The well-worn key slipped easily into the keyhole, sliding the bolt with a greased click. Rebecca gripped the doorknob. The brass was cold to the touch but turned smoothly. Just a push and the door rode inward on its hinges. A wave of freezing air whooshed out. The cold settled on her cheeks and hands while she stood, shivering on the doorstep. *Come on! What will the neighbors think?* Refusing to glance over her shoulder to see if anyone was watching, she went in, closing and locking the door behind her.

The house trembled slightly as the air conditioner labored, pumping out the cold. Rebecca kept her coat on and went quickly past the staircase and straight to the kitchen. Tea. Maybe toast and an egg, but hot tea at least. Rebecca fried an egg and made toast. Sure enough, the rain started again, tapping on the kitchen window and while the kettle worked up to a boil, Rebecca watched the rain make little silver snake paths on the glass. It was too dark to see the backyard where the roses bloomed. Would the rain knock the petals off? Dumb. The roses closed at night. Rebecca turned the egg.

The Earl Grey warmed her, and she needed the food because she ate all of it before making a second cup of tea. After clearing away the dishes, she carefully washed and dried her hands, set the teacup on the table, then took out the library book.

The book was small, an octavo, truly battered with age, and fraying along the edges. Rebecca brushed the worn leather binding with her fingertips -pigskin? The leather looked strange with noticeable pores; little pinpricks scattered like smallpox scars across the cover surface.

After a careful sip of tea, she opened the book. Inside was more skin, delicately yellowed vellum that cracked and rustled like autumn leaves, but it was the ink and the writing that gave Rebecca pause. The ink was wrong, too dark for iron gall ink, maybe red at some point in time, but now, almost black. The writing, now, that was something. The script flowed across the pages in spider strokes.

Though handwritten, the book wasn't a journal. It seemed to be a set of instructions, almost like a recipe book. Rebecca turned back to the first page, the page that caught her attention in the library. She read the title out loud. "To Render the Flesh to Its Essential Salts".

Rebecca knew what Essential Salts were from a weird tale in her lost Arkham collection. In the story, an alchemist took a human body, put it through a magical process that broke the tissue down to something like salt. They collected this salt and used it to find hidden treasure or long-lost occult knowledge.

Rebecca turned the pages. Scrawled throughout were pentacles, astrological symbols, number tables, and bizarre patterns that made her dizzy as she traced them with her eyes. It was a recipe book of sorts – a sorcerer's cookbook.

"So, you're a grimoire," she said aloud. The house shuddered and Rebecca started, glancing up at the ceiling. Just the A/C kicking in again. The electric bill would kill her.

"No!" The shout surprised her. She took a deep breath and reached for the teacup. "No," she said again softly and took a sip. The tea was cold. Pushing the cup safely across the table, she went back to the book.

The text, written in archaic English and Latin, also contained short paragraphs scattered throughout in an odd, guttural language she didn't recognize. At one of these paragraphs, the ink flowed thickly, and the writer had pressed down so hard that the pen had torn through the vellum. As this phrase recurred in several places throughout the text, she tried sounding out the words. "Y'AI NG NGAH, YOG-SOTHOTH H'EE L'GEB F'AI THRODOG UAAAH!"

Rebecca smiled. They were nonsense words. Just a bunch of letters strung together. Like most books on magic, this one was undoubtedly gobbledygook. Still, what if it worked? Maybe there was a little science mixed in. If she could weed that out, then maybe, maybe. Outside, the rain quickened, riding a wind that battered the roses.

After making a whole pot of tea, Rebecca got a pad and pencil and sat down again to read. She would read the book straight through, taking notes. The book wasn't that long, and after all, it was Friday. She had the weekend to rest. Well, catch some sleep on the couch, anyway. Besides, this book had to have some point to it. A prominent family had donated it and a bunch of medical books and papers belonging to a certain Dr. Willet.

Strange though, how Willet's people had dumped all his stuff. The letter accompanying the donation said they wanted the library to 'please take it without question and do with it as deemed fit'. Kind of cruel to the memory of a family member. Of course, people often did that sort of thing. When someone died, the surviving members quickly sold, donated, or even threw away the dead person's property. Usually, it was to get the deceased's house on the market as quickly as possible for the cash. Guilt was what made them 'donate' books to libraries. Rebecca's job was to sort through the donations, but she wasn't a librarian like Mom, just an assistant.

Rebecca rubbed her eyes. That was Jack's fault too, dammit! Mom hadn't said much when she heard of the engagement, but Rebecca knew. *It's okay, Mom. I'll get my library degree after we settle down.* Uh-huh. Right. Mom got her a job though, and working together for that last year was the best.

Rebecca read through the night, until half frozen, she turned the last page. A final line written in Latin said something about biting the dragon's tail, a little dragon drawn underneath. Her Latin was a little rusty, but the meaning no doubt had to do with the whole plan of the book. On the third page was a larger picture of the dragon, cleverly twined around itself like Celtic knotwork. The dragon's head curved around so that it almost bit its own tail. The incantations hinged around invocation of the dragon's head. The twisted body was the process for preparing a cadaver, so the tail part probably meant the conclusion -flesh turned to salt.

Morning sunlight gleamed through the window. Rebecca rose, pacing back and forth in the little kitchen. She bit her knuckles as she paced. The process. My God, the process! Could she go through with it? As the sun warmed the house, the air conditioner kicked on for the hundredth time. Rebecca stopped in front of the window. Outside in the backyard, rose petals lay scattered, torn by the storm. Tears started in her red-rimmed eyes. Turning off the light, she went into the living room and rolled herself in a blanket on the couch.

In the dream, she was the woman in green velvet. The long train of her dress rustled as she ascended a staircase. The staircase went up and up and everything else was darkness except the steps in front of her, lit by a glowing candle that she carried in one hand. Her other hand clutched something smooth and slippery, but she didn't dare look down to see what it was because just one false step and she would fall. Up she climbed until she came to a door that opened into a lavishly dressed bedroom. The candlelight grew brighter in her hand, illuminating a four-poster bed draped with curtains.

Rebecca crossed to the bed, and the curtain drew aside as if blown by a breeze. Lying at rest on the bed was Jack, his face pale, but peaceful -handsome even. Rebecca set the candlestick down on a nightstand next to an empty whiskey bottle. Along the edge of the bed at her feet were more bottles, lined up like soldiers standing on guard. She moved close, careful not to upset the bottles.

Rebecca leaned over, bending as if to kiss Jack's gently smiling lips. Instead, she reached out to ease the plastic bag she carried, over his head. The bag slipped smoothly, gliding past the pillow under his resting head, sliding easily over his face. Jack didn't stir and it was effortless to bring the heavy plastic of the oversized bag down over his chin, past his neck, to rest just above his shoulders.

The zip tie, a bright-yellow little snake, was also easy, and snugged up click by click to dig softly into Jack's Adams apple. Then the bag began to rise and fall, deflating and inflating with each breath until the plastic fogged, blurring Jack's face inside. Rebecca, still minding the bottles, began to step back when a hand shot out and caught the heavy green fabric of her gown. She knocked over bottles, fighting to pull away. The gripping hand drew her down until she was inches from the head in the bag. The bag no longer rose and fell, but instead, filled slowly with pumping vomit.

Rebecca sat bolt upright, coughing, gasping for breath. After a moment, her breathing calmed, and her heart stopped pounding. Morning light slanted into the living room. Rubbing her stiff neck, Rebecca rose, went downstairs to the bathroom, then headed into the kitchen to make a late breakfast. The book still sat on the table. It was Saturday. There was a lot of work to do.

Mom loved to cook in the best Julia Child style. In the kitchen there were quite an assortment of knives, cleavers, and several large boiling pots and roasting pans. After a quick breakfast, Rebecca prepared the kitchen. She set four large pots to boil on the stove, then pushed the table up against a wall and rolled up the rug. On the hardwood floor with a piece of chalk, she traced one of the symbols in the book -an oddly skewed pentagram. Around this, she carefully drew symbols -moons, stars, crosses, single Hebrew and Greek letters along with fragmented phrases from the unknown language. After dusting the chalk off her hands, she laid out a meat cleaver and several of the sharpest knives she could find, then rolled them up in a kitchen towel. Tucking the towel under one arm, she went through the living room and started up the stairs.

The master bedroom wasn't as fancy as the one in her dream. The four-poster bed was there, but no curtains. Jack's rigid body lay in plain sight. Rebecca set the rolled towel and knives on the nightstand after first removing a whiskey bottle. The room was freezing, and she felt relieved to think that she could finally turn off the A/C. Only two days had passed. There was no smell, except for a faint odor of alcohol. She thought about opening the window, but then decided not to in case anyone passing outside might hear. Hear what? What the book said, she had to do. But she couldn't do it here on Mom's bed. Where then? The bathtub.

Jack was a small man, but it took every ounce of Rebecca's strength to drag him off the bed by the ankles, pull him across the floor to the adjoining bathroom, then hoist him into the tub. When first she pulled the body off the bed, it didn't fall like a bag of wet cement. The corpse still had some rigor mortis stiffness to it and remained straight as a board until it hit the floor headfirst. She fled the room when that happened, and it was several minutes before she was able to go back in.

The pots down in the kitchen, big as they were, would be coming to a boil soon, so she needed to work fast. Still, it took a good fifteen minutes to get him to the bathroom. The body stubbornly refused to bend around the corner from the bathroom door to the tub, so she had to jerk at it, sometimes slipping down onto her bottom as she pulled. Finally, sweat pouring down her face, she heaved him into the tub. The corpse seemed to relax. Rebecca watched in horror as Jack slowly settled into the tub. Despite the turkey basting bag over his head, he looked comfortable. Then she realized she would have to undress him.

Rebecca went downstairs and turned off the burners under the boiling pots. The pots looked too much like witches' cauldrons, especially in a room with a pentagram drawn on the floor. Rebecca went over to consult the book propped open on the table. She was delaying the process. She knew it. Dismissing the thought, she consulted the text.

Several edge-curled pages vividly sketched the next steps. Rebecca fought down a rising gorge as she reviewed the drawings. Dr. Willett was no artist if he indeed was the author of the book, but the pictures could easily fit in a copy of *Gray's Anatomy*. Unable to look at the pictures anymore,

Rebecca went to the refrigerator. After gulping some apple juice straight from the container, she put her sweaty hair in a ponytail using a rubber band, then she spied the scissors. Of course, just cut the clothes off. Easy peasy! With a light step, she went back upstairs.

Jack's flesh cut nicely thanks to Mom's sharp knives, but the first cut was the hardest. Rebecca closed her eyes tightly after touching the narrow blade of the butcher knife to Jack's naked thigh. She sawed slowly back and forth until the blade gritted against bone. Rebecca released the knife handle and opened her eyes. The knife, buried in the thigh, stood as if it were stuck in a block of cheese. Dizziness washed over her, and her ears began to ring.

"Don't pass out! Don't pass out, you idiot! It's just meat." Gasping, she wiped sweat from her forehead. Her hands were shaking, and she clasped them together, holding them tight in her lap. After a few moments, she reached out to take the knife but paused. Along the lips of the wound where the knife lay buried, it was red, but no blood flowed. Where was the blood? Trembling, she took hold of the knife and sawed back and forth, grating bone. She worked the blade around the thigh and then, as she reached the underside of the leg, a slow trickle appeared. Rebecca watched, fascinated as thick ropes pooled under the leg and inched along the tub towards the drain. The flow increased as she cut the lower portions of the leg. So, the blood had settled in the body, like motor oil in a pan. Rebecca clicked her tongue. She was going to have to bleach the tub.

The work soon exposed a gleaming, tendon-laced thighbone. After pairing the meat from the bone, Rebecca placed the raw chunks into several plastic garbage bags, Jack's cut-up clothes lay piled next to the bags. The legs weren't so bad. She pretended to debone a chicken, and after an hour, Jack was a skeleton from the waist down. The worst part would be chopping the joints with a meat cleaver. She didn't want to chip Mom's tub.

After stripping the legs of flesh, Rebecca took a break. She went down to the kitchen and drank some more juice but couldn't quite bring herself to eat a sandwich. She nibbled a few crackers instead, then got out a big chopping block and went back upstairs.

With the block placed under Jack's knee joint, the tub porcelain was safe from the hacking. The old meat cleaver was still sharp from the last time Mom used it, but it took four solid whacks to cut through the tough knee joint, while the second took only three. Next, the feet needed detached. The ankle bones crunched delicately, and it was not long before feet and shin bones were tucked into bags. Cutting the thighbones clear of the hips was hard work. Rebecca hacked away at the stubborn bone which chipped and cracked under her blows. Her arm felt like lead before she finally got the thighs free, and one clumsy strike sunk deep into the stomach above. A squirt of black blood spattered her face making her cry out. She rushed to the sink and washed herself clean before turning back to the tub.

The stomach contents gleamed through the wound like coiled snakes. Biting her lips, Rebecca switched to the butcher knife. A long incision from belly button to breastbone laid open the rib cage and stomach contents. A noxious stench rose from the guts. Trembling and breathing in short breaths, Rebecca heaved the dripping intestines into a bag, then rooted around in the chest cavity, freeing the heart and lungs with slashes from the knife. After a time, the blood ceased rolling from the body. More hacks with the blade, and a section of ribcage was free. An image of the ribs on a platter decorated with little white paper hats flashed in her mind -Mom's Christmas crown roast.

Two hours later, Rebecca stood up to ease her aching legs and survey her work. All that remained was Jack's head in the bag, still attached to a section of spine. The head had rolled free in the hacking and lay in a pool of black blood in the middle of the tub. Despite her care, blood was everywhere. Blood dried on her hands, right up to her elbows. Glistening blood splashed freely on the edges of the tub and up on the wall behind. Blood smeared from where she knelt covered her pants and blouse. The clothes needed burning and she desperately wanted a bath, but first, the head.

Even though she had just butchered her husband into quivering chunks, Rebecca was reluctant to take the bag off the head. The job was necessary according to the book. Clothing, jewelry, or any other material hampered the transformation. She couldn't do it. Not yet. Instead, she closed her eyes down to slits, lifted the head, and dropped it into a garbage bag.

Cleaning up was horrible. Rebecca wasted three more hours mopping up blood and bleaching the tub. She slipped out of her clothes and put them in a bag with Jack's. Shyly naked, she hauled the heavy bags on several trips down to the kitchen, then returned to the bathroom to bathe. Rebecca scoured herself roughly in icy water, kneeling in the tub. She couldn't bring herself to stretch out and soak, resting against the enamel where Jack's body so recently lay. Finally, freshly dressed, Rebecca made herself a sandwich which she ate in the living room. Her body ached and she felt like taking a nap, but the day was passing, and the afternoon sunlight slanted warmly into the room. It was time to render the flesh.

The pots were set to boil once again, but Rebecca needed one more thing to start the process -saltpeter. Potassium nitrate was a preservative, but Rebecca remembered that it was a primary chemical used to make fireworks. In the Special Collections at the library, an old book described Chinese alchemists using Saltpeter which 'burned with a purple flame' to create 'fires in the sky'. Rebecca hunted through every cupboard in the kitchen and found the other necessary ingredients for the process -basil, chamomile, lavender, oil of clove. Earlier, out in the rain-damp garden, she had cut some rosemary and then ground the whole mix in a mortar, so everything was ready except the saltpeter. Leaning wearily against the sink, Rebecca stared out the window. Outside, the weeping willows long, green tendrils swayed in the wind. Behind the tree was the garden shed. Rebecca hurried outside.

Glistening cobwebs draped the shed. Rebecca pulled open the creaking door and went in, brushing webs from her face. On a shelf piled with rusting garden tools were several packets of seeds and a green cardboard box of Miracle Grow, broken open by the damp. Rebecca lifted the box, careful not to spill the contents from its cracked sides. She ran her finger down the list of ingredients printed in faded ink. There it was potassium nitrate. Rebecca hurried back to the kitchen with her prize.

The shadows of late afternoon stretched across the yard. The pots were once again boiling merrily on the stove. Into these, Rebecca tossed handfuls of the mixture required for the process. She had added the full box of Miracle Grow to the other ground up ingredients, hoping that the plant fertilizer contained enough saltpeter. After stirring the contents in each pot, she reluctantly began pulling the grisly contents from the plastic bags. Into a roasting cauldron, she arranged the broken long bones -femurs, tibia, and fibula, alongside radius, ulna, and the remaining arm bones. After fussing a bit with the bones, she popped the whole thing in the oven. On the stovetop in two deep pots, mounds of flesh bubbled in the boil. In another, the feet stewed with the hands, chopped-up ribs, and other fragments. On the last burner, Mom's favorite soup pot stood ready.

Taking short, gasping breaths, Rebecca eased the blood-sticky head out of the garbage bag. Slowly, hands trembling, she pulled free the yellow zip tie and slid the basting bag off Jack's head. The head sat balanced heavily on the palm of her hand; one eye closed in a wink, the other half open, the blue iris slightly glazed. The mouth sagged open, an ooze of brown vomit coated the lips and chin. Rebecca began to retch, her whole body shaking. The head dropped, hit the floor, and rolled, coming to rest near the table. Rebecca raced outside into the garden and threw up her lunch.

Rebecca walked in slow circles, mumbling to herself. "It has to be done. It must be done. Come on you fool, finish the job." When her heart stopped thudding in her chest, Rebecca wiped cold sweat from her face and went back inside. Jack's head, brown hair hanging lank, sat propped against a table leg. Moaning softly, Rebecca went over, stepping so not to smudge the chalk pentagram on the floor, and picked up the head. In a trance, she went to the stove and dropped the head into the soup pot. The head bobbed in the steaming water. Rebecca put a lid on the pot and went into the living room. She curled herself into a tight ball on the couch and went to sleep.

Midnight. The house was quiet. Rebecca stretched, then massaged her aching neck. A dull headache thumped in her temples. Back in the kitchen, she drank three glasses of water, then checked on the pots, topping them off with water and the last bit of the spices. She eased the soup pot lid off just enough to pour in some more water without seeing what simmered inside. A full twenty hours, that's what the book said. After twenty hours of boiling, top off with water and remaining ingredients, then cook down to the essence. What the 'essence' was, Rebecca didn't know, but it must be the flesh and fat rendered until no moisture remained. The book showed a picture that wasn't clear, a pile of something mounded in the center of the pentagram.

Late as it was, Rebecca ate, then took a bath. This time, she lay back in the clean tub, resting in the warm water. After the bath, she stripped the bed, made it fresh with clean sheets, and went to sleep under the covers. Hours later, she woke to the smell of burning.

Blue smoke curled from around the oven door. Grabbing an oven mitt, Rebecca eased the oversized roasting pan out of the oven and placed it on the counter. Scorched black, the bones inside had cooked to crumbling charcoal. While the bones cooled, she propped open the kitchen door to let in some air and clear the smoke. She prayed there wasn't enough to alert the neighbors.

The boil worked. The contents of each pot had cooked down to a gray pudding. Rebecca stirred the contents of each with a wooden spoon and adjusted the burners to low heat. Another hour or two of careful simmering, and all that would remain was a crusty powder. The pot with the head was another matter. Steeling herself for what was inside, Rebecca removed the lid. Success. The skull was clean of flesh. The eyes had dropped from the sockets and melted in the sludge. Using oven mitts, Rebecca lifted the steaming skull out of the pot and set it on the counter. She gave the remaining contents a good stir, then turned the heat to low to let it finish.

The skull still had fragments of tendon clinging to it. A patch of hair plastered wetly, clung to one side. Rebecca removed the blackened bones from the roasting pan and placed them on a platter. She put the skull in the pan, and slipped it into the oven, set it to broil. She would have to risk the smoke. The book said the bones must blacken but could remain whole if placed properly for the ritual. Rebecca set a kitchen timer for two hours, then made a frugal breakfast which she took outside to eat in the garden.

Sunday breakfast in the garden. Rebecca munched a piece of toast and admired the roses. Red, pink, and white blooms nodded in the morning breeze. Gardening, cooking, and books, that was Mom. Rebecca remembered the pride Mom took in all three. She was sitting at a little wrought iron table with matching chairs. Before her marriage, she and Mom had enjoyed many breakfasts at this table.

Rebecca raised her glass of orange juice to the empty chair. "To you, Mom. I toast you." The raised glass trembled as she held it. "Forgive me," she whispered, and set it down with a click. She took a deep breath and glanced around the garden, at the willow tree, the little shed, the ivy-covered wall that protected it all. "You're all I have left, and that's fine. That's fine!" Laughing, she cleared the breakfast things and went in to check the roasting skull.

Two hours passed quickly. Rebecca periodically checked the heat. While she waited, she read. The book was a paperback called *The Monk,* by Matthew Lewis. The gothic romance written in the late 1700's, spun a tale around the corruption of the monk, Ambrosio and the virtue of a maiden, Antonia. Rebecca was buried deep in the novel's lurid descriptions when the timer went off.

The skull was black, the remnants of hair and tendon shriveled in the fierce heat. The rendered flesh was also ready, and Rebecca scraped the contents of each pot into a steaming pile in the center of the chalk pentagram. At each of the five pentacle points, she laid the bones. To the east the arm bones lay crossed, to the west, the legs. The delicate hands and feet rested in the southeast point, while the ribs, pelvis bones and spine sat piled to the southwest. Lastly, Rebecca set Jack's skull in the northernmost point of the symbol, then consulted the book. The passage she wanted was near the end, written on a page sprinkled with old blood.

And so, the drawing of the five into one shall set the stars in motion. Speak to Azathoth. Speak to Tsathoggua. Cry out across the Empty Space to draw them.

Y'AI NG NGAH, YOG-SOTHOTH H'EE L'GEB F'AI THRODOG UAAAH!

Whisper to Dagon, Master of the Depths, and echo the command to Yibb-Tstll in rustling green. Let voice cascade across the boiling sea to unseal the vaults of R'Lyeh.

PH'NGLUI MGLW'NAFH CTHULHU R'LYEH WGAH'NAGL FHATGN!

Time to begin. Rebecca selected a small knife, a favorite for paring apples, from the nearly empty knife drawer. She laid the knife in front of the propped open book, then turned the pages back to the beginning of the spoken part of the process -the spell for making Essential Salts.

The spell didn't take long to recite, but Rebecca labored slowly over the strange words. Her voice rang hollow in the kitchen, sometimes rising, sometimes falling to a whisper. The sun began to dim as if a cloud passed over. The air grew cold. Rebecca hesitated, thinking that maybe the A/C was on again, but she couldn't worry about that now. It was time to offer a sacrifice.

Rebecca squared her shoulders and lifted the paring knife. She gritted her teeth, then made two quick cross-shaped slices in the palm of her left hand. Breathing heavily, she clenched her fist, holding it over the book. A trickle of blood welled from her fingers and dripped, falling on the pages -a sprinkling of blood to draw the gods. Shaking off the pain, Rebecca turned a page, then froze. The room took on a blueish glow, and behind her, a horrible sound.

Rebecca faced the book on the table, her back to the bone-laden pentagram. She turned quickly and gasped. The bones were moving. Down the arms of the five-pointed star, the arm and leg bones slid. The skeletal hands crawled like inchworms, while the feet shuffled forward. They were edging their way inwards, towards the rendered flesh in the center. The gray sludge pulsed and writhed, glowing blue. As Rebecca watched, eyes wide, Jack's grinning skull rolled to join the bones, coming to a stop on top of the pile where it sat as though waiting.

Rebecca forced herself to turn back to the book. She leaned against the kitchen table, then reached out and turned the next to the last page. Swallowing, she croaked the words that spoke of the dragon turning its head to gaze at its tail. As the last words died in her dry throat, the room flashed with light, and a smell like burning sulfur choked her. A popping sound like a childhood breakfast cereal 'snap, crackle, pop', made her turn after catching her breath.

In the center of the pentagram was a pile of silver-white dust. The powder clicked and snapped as tiny crystals formed, glittering like ice chips.

Stepping forward, Rebecca cautiously stirred the dust with the toe of her shoe. Bones, flesh, and skull had vanished. "Ashes to ashes, dust to dust."

Rebecca danced. Around the salts she danced, throwing her arms up, jumping, and spinning, until she almost fell with dizziness. Tears were on her cheeks and her nose started to run. She wiped her face with her sleeve.

"We did it, Mom! We did it! I'm gonna... I'm gonna get my books back and I'll get everything back, and, and, I'll get my degree, and everything will be like it was!"

Rebecca pounded the kitchen table with her fists, laughing. The grimoire slid to one side, partly turning a page.

"Oh, you beautiful book!" Rebecca reached out to right the tome, then paused. There was a sentence written on the last tattered page. Drawn below the script, the familiar dragon now bit its own tail. "Oh hell, that's right, there's more." Leaning over to read, Rebecca ran her finger along the last line, sounding out the Latin words. "'Et mordeat draco cauda sua. Redierit quod coepit.' The dragon bites its tail. All returns as it began." She straightened, frowning. "What does that mean?"

A sigh. A long, drawn-out sigh.

Rebecca spun around.

Jack sat naked in the smudged pentagram.

Rebecca fell back against the table.

"Hey 'Becca. You cookin' somethin'?" Jack smiled faintly, then looked down, eyebrows lifting. "Where's my clothes?"

"You… you were in the tub."

Jack rubbed his legs. "Yeah? Well, it's freezing down here. Damn, I'm cold. I could use a drink." He struggled clumsily to his feet.

Rebecca shook her head from side to side. A tingle crept along her scalp, numbness in her lips, then a whining buzz. Darkness started at the edges of her vision. Through the blurring, Rebecca saw Jack's face come close, a smiling head. Behind her, the kitchen table pressed against her hips. She turned away and leaned against the table. The old book was still there. Mom's sharp little paring knife rested beside it.

**

The men stood peering through the grated window of the cell door. The older of the two, a man with a grey, pointed beard, cleared his throat. "No change then?"

The other man who wore a guard's uniform, shook his head. "Just the same. She's a model prisoner."

"Well, if she keeps it up, she'll be out on probation in six months."

The warden chuckled.

"What?"

"Well, she won't be happy about that. She seems to like it here."

The prison psychologist stroked his beard, tugging at the point. "That's what I don't like. It wasn't wise putting her in solitary. She should be with other inmates some of the time. The isolation feeds her psychosis."

"She helps out in the prison library. In fact, we've considered keeping her on as librarian. She knows her stuff. Even completed a full librarian degree while in here. All online of course."

The psychologist peered through the grate. Inside, the woman sat at a tiny desk, reading. Several books sat piled next to her.

"Can't imagine her doing what she did. What did they say, some kind of witchcraft ritual?"

The psychologist stepped away from the door and put his hands in his pockets. "That's what the police found. The kitchen all chalked with occult symbols and him lying nude with his throat slashed."

"Weird, but what isn't nowadays?" The warden took a last look at the girl before closing the grate. Inside, Rebecca turned a page and continued to read, a smile curving her lips.

A Journey with Charon

I stood alone on a shattered flint shore. The broad water ran smoothly, at my feet. Across the river deepened darkness while above and somehow behind, a faded twilight broken by the flickering Dog Star. There was no bridge across the river but just as I began to turn back, I saw a light upon the water. A lantern light hanging from the prow of a long-hulled boat which turned, coming to rest before me. Without a pause, I stepped aboard.

The man stretched out his bone-thin arm, palm strangely cupped. I reached to take the gnarled hand, but he shook his head.

"Obol... You must make the offering," he whispered.

A copper taste flooded my mouth. From under my tongue, I took the bitter coin and placed it in his upturned palm. With a nod, he pointed to a low bench at the center of the boat. I sat facing forward and we pulled away into deeper water.

I imagine some passengers looking anxiously ahead to see if there is any light beyond the lantern. Others might be distraught and restless, moving about or even jumping out to slide beneath the rolling depths. I tell myself to sit straight and still so as not to tip the boat. I don't look ahead, but down to watch the passing flood.

That water was the blackest ink where an endless tale of life was written slipping past the skimming eye. Mists rose from the parchment flood, and I stretched out my hand to somehow stop that endless sorrow but drew back when a sinuous hand rose up to meet my own. More followed, pale arms with spider-like fingers reaching, sliding along the surface of the boat. Waterweed caught on some outstretched arms which glowed in their own corpse light, but soon we passed beyond those souls waving in final farewell.

The boat made a sudden turn, steering for an outthrust spit of rock. For the first, I felt afraid and tried to rise, but the boat pulled alongside the waiting figure.

"Salutes Mortem," the Pilot said and for a moment, a smile shaped his lips.

The figure was as he always had been -cloaked and hooded in rags, he gripped the gunwale with skeletal fingers and stepped aboard. I edged away, trapped between those unwelcome two. The passenger sat facing me, below the upswept prow. His face a gleam of bone, the death's head and yet, instead of empty sockets, he watches me with eyes the deepest blue.

"Would you dare speak?" That voice which one never wants to hear was rich and strong and where I was ready at once to hide my face in my hands, I found myself looking up into those eyes that watched me and in a moment I felt that look upon me and that voice that spoke were at once gentle and my heart quickened for a moment hoping that perhaps the passenger was not there for me after all but even as this thought came, just as quickly did my hope fail and he spoke on.

"There was a time when those I met would reach across to embrace me believing that I would take them beyond the Sleepless Isle and into the arms of lovers lost. Some made bold demands to be taken back, some holding out the science key, while fewer still who in all humility sought the One who Saves and resurrection rest at journey's end.

But this day most do what they did for all that time before. . . nothing. And you?"

I confess that when I heard this question, I had no reply. Tears started in my eyes because of it. Was I one of those who did nothing? It seemed the greatest sorrow of all if it were true. The horrid waste of doing, of believing, of following, of desiring nothing. Even the greatest depth of corruption seemed more easily forgivable than such squandering of one's existence. A gift ignored. And so, I started to cry and said, "As you are right now, I will be soon enough, and I deserve it." After I bit, I looked into those strangely blue eyes and suddenly knew. That fleshless face which one would expect to have no means of showing emotion, was filled with sadness. I knew at that very moment of Death's own despair, but I also realized that from it flowed compassion. And then in a rush, I felt hope and remembered that it was how I had spent my time before, always with some hope. Even at the worst I'd had a little and it was still with me now.

"So, you see it then?" he asked, nodding slightly. "You recognize it? Well then drink this." And from beneath his cloak, he took a silver chalice wrought with a delicate filagree traced like the web of spiders.

I took the chalice and saw that it was filled with what looked like water, clear as crystal.

"Drink then," he said.

As I drank the water, pure and cold at first, but then warmed in my mouth and throat and seemed to turn into the richest of wines, red as newly spilt blood, but I drank on and finished the cup and handed it back to him. He nodded and his eyes glinted like sapphires. Then he settled back in his seat, drawing his hood over his face as in sleep.

Charon rowed without pause and the dark water slipped away. I sat looking ahead on a journey of my own.

About the Author

Don Cleave has taught Shakespeare and Gothic literature as a professor of English and given lectures on the occult, exorcism, and horror fiction. A true book fanatic, Don collects ghost stories and other works on the supernatural. He is also a founding member of The West Coast Writer's Coven, a group of sci-fi, fantasy, and horror writers. Don's greatest passion outside of books is sharing real adventures with his wife and children on the mist shrouded beaches of the haunted West Coast.